Note to Parents

On the Go!, Level 3 of the *Now I'm Reading!*™ series, has five "just right" stories that use a step-by-step early reading approach. The stories in Level 3 integrate the short- and long-vowel sounds introduced in Levels 1 and 2 with more phonics skills, additional sight words, word endings, digraphs, consonant blends, and double consonants.

Story 1 is the easiest and story 5 is the most challenging. For optimum success, have your child read the stories in sequence the first few times. After that, as your child grows more comfortable with the various skills, he or she can read the stories in any order.

For more information on how to use these stories with your child, refer to the pages at the end of this book.

NOW I'M READING!™

ON THE GO!

LEVEL 3 ■ VOLUME 2

Written by Nora Gaydos
Illustrated by BB Sams

Hardcover Bind-up Edition
copyright © 2002, 2006 by innovativeKids®
All rights reserved
Published by innovativeKids®
A division of innovative USA®, Inc.
18 Ann Street
Norwalk, CT 06854
Printed in China

Conceived, developed, and designed
by the creative team at innovativeKids®
www.innovativekids.com

For permission to use any
part of this publication, contact
innovativeKids®
Phone: 203-838-6400
Fax: 203-855-5582
E-mail: info@innovativekids.com

Table of Contents

TY IN THE SKY

Skills in this story: Vowel sounds: short and long vowels; Word ending: *-ing*;
Initial consonant blends: *pl, fl, tr, sk, st*; Y as a vowel: *y* says *i*

Ty wants to fly. Ty wants to fly in the sky.

The sky is dry. The sky is dry
so Ty can fly with Sly.

The plane is going up in the sky.
Ty is going to fly in the sky with Sly.

Time goes by. "I want to try to fly," said Ty.

"I want to fly the plane!" said Ty.
"Do not cry," said Sly. "You can fly."

Oh my! Ty is trying to fly. Ty is trying
to fly the plane in the sky.

Good try! The plane is flying
up in the sky.

"My oh my," screams Ty,
"where is the sky?"

Now Ty is NOT flying the plane
in the sky. Why?

Ty, Sly, and the plane are in
a pig sty!

SLOW THE BOAT

Skills in this story: Vowel sounds: short and long vowels; Vowel followed by r: *ar;* Vowel followed by w: *ow;* Word ending: *-ing;* Initial consonant blends: *st, sl, cr;* Final consonant blends: *nd, ld*

■ ■

Jo and Mo own a boat.
Jo and Mo own a rowboat.

Jo and Mo like to row. Jo and Mo like to row the boat slow.

Oh, no! The wind is starting to blow.

The waves are starting to grow.

Jo and Mo are not going slow.
They are not going slow in their rowboat.

Oh, no! Jo and Mo are not
rowing the boat anymore.

Jo and Mo see some crows. Jo and Mo hope the crows can slow the boat.

The crows see the bow on Jo.
"Give us your bow," say the crows.

The crows tie Jo's bow to the rowboat.
The crows hold the bow.

The crows hold the bow to slow
the boat for Jo and Mo.

OH BOY, ROY

Skills in this story: Vowel sounds: short and long vowels; Initial consonant digraph: *ch;* Initial consonant blends: *cl, sl, sp;* Vowel digraphs: *oy, oi*

■ ■

"My bike is not a toy,"
said Roy to the boys.

Roy cleaned the coils.

Roy cleaned the coils
and added the oil.

The boys looked at Roy
as he rode off with joy.

Roy saw a coin in the soil.
"Oh boy," said Roy.

Roy made a bad choice.
Roy slid on the soil.

Roy slid on the soil. The bike
leaked oil.

The bike went over the soil and leaked oil. The bike made a big noise.

Roy pointed to his bike. The bike was spoiled with soil and oil.

Roy pointed to the coin.
The coin was just a bit of foil!

THE WIND BLEW

BLEW

Skills in this story: Vowel sounds: short and long vowels; Vowel followed by r: *ar*;
Vowel followed by w: *ew;* Initial consonant digraph: *th;* Initial consonant blends: *bl, gr, fl gl, sc;*
Double consonant: *ss*

Drew got into the jeep. Drew got into the new jeep for a ride.

Drew threw the top off the new jeep.

Drew went down the street in the
new jeep. He went by a road crew.

Drew went by a few goats. Drew
went by a few goats chewing food.

Then the wind blew.
The wind blew and grew.

The wind blew and Drew's hat flew.

The wind grew and Drew's glasses flew.

The wind grew and Drew's
scarf flew.

Drew grew blue. Drew ran over the dew on the grass to get the things that blew.

The goats wore all the things
that flew!

■ STORY 5 ■

DAWN DRAWS

Skills in this story: Vowel sounds: short and long vowels; Vowel followed by w: *aw;*
Word ending: *-ed;* Initial consonant digraph: *sh;* Initial consonant blends: *dr, tr, st, cl, str*

■ ■

Dawn got on a train with Shawn.
Dawn got on the train to draw
what she saw.

Dawn looked out at the straw. "I will draw what is on the straw," said Dawn.

Dawn saw a big yawn. "I will draw
the big yawn," said Dawn.

Dawn saw paws. "I will draw the paws that I saw on the straw," said Dawn.

Dawn saw claws. "I will draw
the sharp claws," said Dawn.

Dawn saw jaws. "I will draw
the jaws eating straw," said Dawn.

The train stopped. Dawn and Shawn
stepped on the lawn.

"Look what I saw," said Dawn.

"I saw a big yawn, paws, claws, and jaws."

"I saw all of that on the straw," said Dawn, "and look what else I saw!"

▪ ▪ ▪ ▪ ▪ How to Use This Book ▪ ▪ ▪ ▪ ▪

Prepare by reading the stories ahead of time.
Familiarize yourself with the skills reinforced in each story. By doing this, you can better guide your child in recognizing the new words and sounds as they appear in the text.

Before reading, look at the pictures with your child.
Encourage him or her to tell the story through the pictures. Next, read the books aloud to your child. Point to the words as you read to promote a connection between the spoken word and the printed word.

Have your child read to you. Encourage him or her to point to the words as he or she reads. By doing so, your child will begin to understand that each word has a separate sound and is represented in a distinct way on the page.

Encourage your child to read independently. This is the ultimate goal. Have him or her read alone or read aloud to other family members and friends.

▪ ▪

After You Read Activities

To help reinforce comprehension of the story:
- Ask your child simple questions about the story, such as "What does Ty want to try?" (from *Ty in the Sky*).
- Ask questions that require an understanding of the story, such as "Where does Ty land the plane?"

To reinforce phonetic vowel sounds:
- Ask your child to say words that rhyme with each other and have the same vowel sound, such as *sky* and *fly*.

To reinforce understanding of words and sentences:
- Pick out two or three words from the story and have your child use all of them in a sentence.
- Pick out a sentence from a story and scramble the words. Then ask your child to unscramble the words to form a real sentence. For example: *Ty to is fly. trying*

To help develop imagination:
- Ask your child to make up a story using his or her favorite characters from the book.
- Write the story down and have your child draw pictures to go with the story.

■ ■ ■ **The Now I'm Reading!**™ **Series** ■ ■ ■

The *Now I'm Reading!*™ series integrates the best of phonics and literature-based reading. Phonics emphasizes letter-sound relationships, while a literature-based approach brings the enjoyment and excitement of a real story. The series has six reading levels:

Pre-Reader: Children "read" simple, patterned, and repetitive text and use picture clues to help them along.

Level 1: Children learn short vowel sounds, simple consonant sounds, and common sight words.

Level 2: Children learn long and short vowel sounds, more consonants and consonant blends, plus more sight word reinforcement.

Level 3: Children learn new vowel sounds, with more consonant blends, double consonants, and longer words and sentences.

Level 4: Children learn advanced word skills, including silent letters, multi-syllable words, compound words, and contractions.

Independent: Children are introduced to high-interest topics as they tackle challenging vocabulary words and information by using previous phonics skills.

■ ■ ■ ■ ■ ■ ■ ■ ■ ■ ■ ■ ■ ■ ■ ■ ■ ■ ■ ■

Glossary of Terms

Phonics: The use of letter-sound relationships to help youngsters identify written words.

Sight Words: Frequently used words, recognized automatically on sight, which do not require decoding, such as *a, the, is,* and so on.

Decoding: Breaking a word into parts, giving each letter or letter combination its corresponding sound, and then pronouncing the word (sometimes called "sounding out").

Consonant Letters: Letters that represent the consonant sounds and, except *Y,* are not vowels—*B, C, D, F, G, H, J, K, L, M, N, P, Q, R, S, T, V, W, X, Y, Z.*

Short Vowels: The vowel sounds similar to the sound of *a* in *cat, o* in *dog, i* in *pig, u* in *cub,* and *e* in *hen.*

Long Vowels: The vowel sounds that are the same as the names of the alphabet letters *a, e, i, o,* and *u.* Except for *y,* long-vowel words have two vowels in them. They either have a silent *e* at the end of the word (for example *home*), or they use a vowel pattern or combination, such as *ai, ee, ea, oa, ue,* and so on.

Consonant Blend: A sequence of two or more consonants in a word, each of which holds its distinct sound when the word is pronounced. Consonant blends can occur at the beginning or at the end of a word—as in <u>sl</u>ip or la<u>st</u> or <u>str</u>eet.

Consonant Digraph: A combination of two consonant letters that represent a single speech sound, which is different from either consonant sound alone. Consonant digraphs can occur at the beginning or the end of a word—as in <u>sh</u>ip or fi<u>sh</u>.

Literature-Based Reading: Using quality stories and books to help children learn to read.

Reading Comprehension: The ability to understand and integrate information from the text that is read. The skill ranges from a literal understanding of a text to a more critical and creative appreciation of it.

About the Author

Nora Gaydos is an elementary school teacher with more than ten years of classroom experience teaching kindergarten, first grade, and third grade. She has a broad understanding of how beginning readers develop from the earliest stage of pre-reading to becoming independent, self-motivated readers. Nora has a degree in elementary education from Miami University in Ohio and lives in Connecticut with her husband and two sons. Nora is also the author of *Now I Know My ABCs* and *Now I Know My 1, 2, 3's*, as well as other early-learning concept books published by innovativeKids®.